Roody Kangaroo
MOVES FORWARD

by John Brubaker   illustrated by Piper Colston

ISBN: 9798826901434

Printed in the United States of America

Cover and interior illustration by Piper Colston

Written and published by: John Brubaker

To order visit: **CUCOroody.com** or call (930) CALL-BRU

Bulk discounts available

Acknowledgments

Many thanks to Rhonda Yaklin for the inspiration to create Roody Kangaroo Moves Forward, and to my amazing illustrator Piper Colston- whose creative mind and artistic talent made this project shine brighter than I ever imagined. Without both of you, none of this would've been possible.

Dedication

To every parent and kid who has ever had to persevere in the face of adversity, challenge, and disappointment; this book is for you.

-John Brubaker

It was Monday morning at Jungletown Elementary.
Roody Kangaroo bounced into the classroom and took
his usual seat in the front row.
Miss Screech the teacher perched on her table.
"We're having a pop quiz!" she said.

The little kangaroo felt confident. He thought he might be the smartest creature in the class. Once the quiz was over, Miss Screech gathered the animals' answers and marked the papers. Soon the wise owl was ready to announce the winner.

"Congratulations India Elephant," said Miss Screech.
"You're top of the class!"
Roody was sad when he saw his score. He hadn't even
finished in second place. The little kangaroo limped home
with his tail between his legs.

"It's not fair!" Roody cried to his parents that evening. "Elephants never forget anything. And I think Streaky Cheetah was cheating on the test."

Roody's mom took his front paw. "Whenever something bad happens, you need to have a kangaroo mindset. Take a deep breath in and then a deep breath out."

"That's right, Roody," said Dad. "Chin up, chest out and move forward. Now go out and play with your friends."

Roody bounced out of the house to find his friends. He looked all over Jungletown. Finally, he found them, sitting on a log.

India Elephant, Streaky Cheetah and Al E. Gator were watching an outdoor movie. Florence Sloth was there too, although she'd fallen asleep. Al E. Gator was laughing at something on the screen.

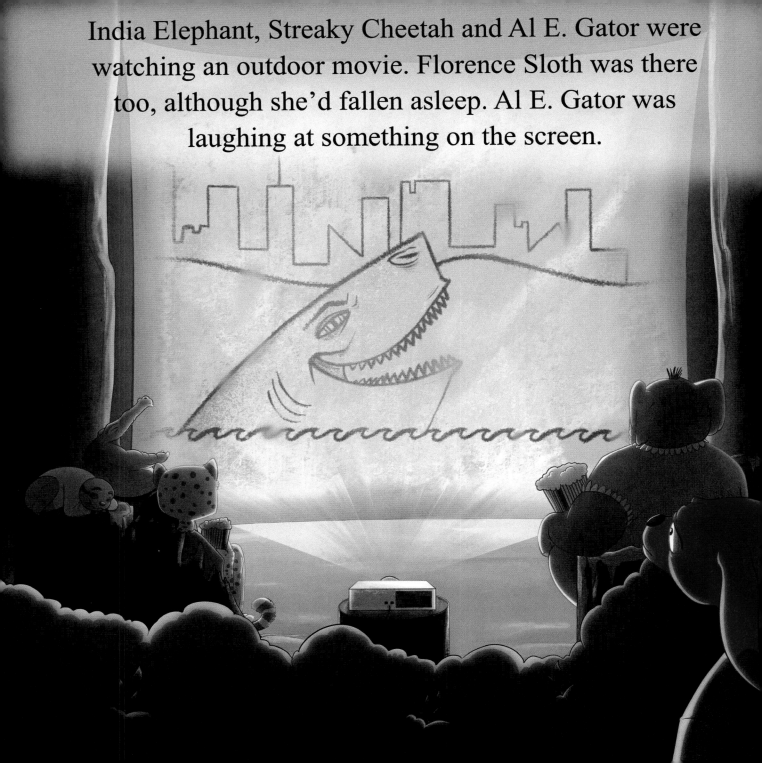

Roody had a strange feeling in his belly. Was he jealous, upset or hopping mad? All his friends had gathered together. Why had nobody told him?

"Why didn't you invite me to the movie?" the kangaroo asked.

"I'm sorry," said Streaky Cheetah, "but we're watching a scary movie, and you are much too jumpy."

Feeling left out, the little kangaroo lost his bounce.
He walked home once again, with his tail between his legs.
"My friends think I'm too jumpy," sighed Roody.
"Well, maybe my jumpiness will impress them at Sports Day

The first event at Sports Day was the sprint. Roody bounced at top speed, using his big back feet to leap forward. The fast kangaroo passed his friends on the running track, leaving them far behind…

All except for Streaky Cheetah, whose top speed was even quicker than the kangaroo's. The cheetah raced past Roody, crossing the finish line before him.

"At least he didn't cheat this time," thought Roody.
"I'll definitely win the next event."

The next event was the high jump! Roody smiled. There was no way that anyone could beat him. The springy kangaroo hopped ten feet in the air, higher than all of his friends. "Woo-HOO!" bounced Roody. "I won the high jump!"

Miss Screech cleared her throat. She pointed to another high jump bar, which was much lower than Roody's.

A tiny green insect was leaping over it!

"This is our new student, Gaudy Grasshopper," said the owl.

"Roody, your jump was five times taller than you are, but Gaudy's leap was twenty times taller than her own height."

Roody couldn't believe it!
He hopped over to his parents, who were
watching the competition.

"It's not fair!" sulked Roody.
"I should have been the winner."
"That doesn't matter," said Mom. "What's
most important is you tried your best."

Dad crouched down beside his son. "You know what's special about us kangaroos? Our big feet cannot walk backwards. That means we always move onto the next challenge. So, chin up, chest out... and move forward."

The next challenge came the following day. Roody's friends invited him to go roller skating in the jungle. As the kangaroo's feet were quite long, Dad made him a special pair of shoes from two skateboards.

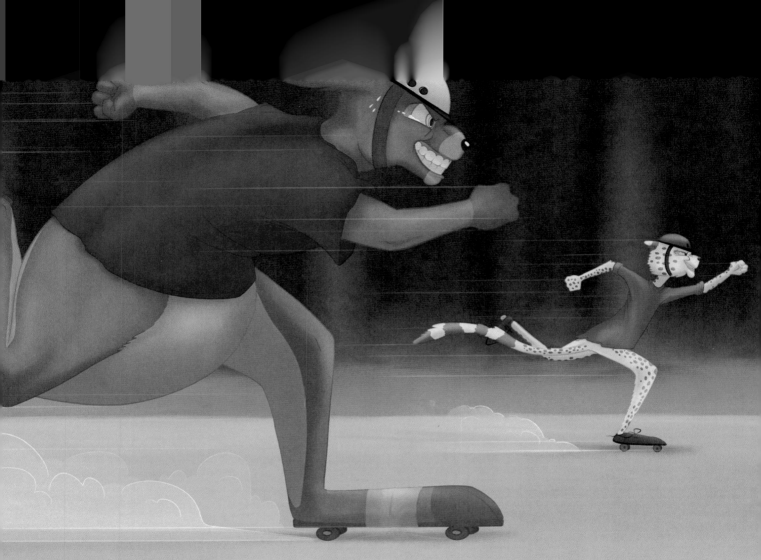

The creatures had loads of fun skating through the trees. Roody
thought he might even beat Streaky Cheetah!
India Elephant blew her trunk.
"Watch OUT!" she shouted. "There's a river straight ahead!"
Streaky Cheetah SCREAMED! He was terrified of water!

Florence Sloth slowed to a stop.
She hadn't been skating very fast in the first place.
"Oh no," yawned the sleepy creature.
"Streaky Cheetah and Roody are racing too fast."
India Elephant flapped her ears in panic. Then, the clever
elephant had an idea.

"Try skating backwards," India trumpeted.
"That will slow you down."
Streaky Cheetah slid his paws backwards and slowed
down just in time. Try as he might,
Roody couldn't move his legs the other way.
The kangaroo rolled straight into the river!

Luckily, the water wasn't too high, and Roody swam to the surface. The soggy kangaroo felt very sorry for himself. Al E. Gator bobbed up beside him in the river. "Nice to see you, Roody," grinned the reptile. "Do you know I can't crawl backwards either? You and I are just the same."

Roody limped home, dripping all the way.
"I hate only moving forward," the cold kangaroo
complained to his parents.
"There's nothing good about it at all. I'm just the same
as a scaly alligator."
Gloomily, Roody went to bed.

The next day was also gloomy. Stormy clouds filled the sky and heavy rain poured down on Jungletown.
Roody went down the hill toward school but found he couldn't bounce any further.
"I must have hopped in the wrong direction," he thought.
Suddenly, Roody heard a familiar SCREAM!

The river had burst its banks! A lot of
the jungle was flooded. Roody could
see Streaky Cheetah, trying to swim in
the swirling water.
"HELP!" cried the terrified cheetah.
The brave kangaroo bounced into the
river.

Streaky Cheetah climbed onto the kangaroo's back. Roody used his large feet to wade out of the rising water. He started to climb toward dry land. Carrying the cheetah was very hard work!

Soon Roody was exhausted, but there was
only one way to safety. As he climbed uphill,
he remembered the kangaroo mindset.
"Chin up, chest out… move forward," repeated Roody.
"Chin up, chest out… move forward… chin up, chest out…"
Finally, Roody reached the top of the hill!

The news of Streaky Cheetah's rescue spread all over Jungletown. When the flood was over, Roody's friends and proud parents gathered at school. There was a big party to celebrate the heroic kangaroo.

Miss Screech invited the happy kangaroo to make a speech.
"Sometimes things happen that you can't control," said
Roody. "You might get a disappointing score or not win a
race. Sometimes you might feel left out. You can't change
the past, but you can make the next day better.
Chin up, chest out and move forward!"

About Roody

Roody The Kangaroo is the official mascot of our clothing brand, *Chin Up Chest Out Apparel*.

Why? Because the kangaroo is the only mammal that can't move backwards.

They symbolize progress, always moving forward.

The inability to move backwards: Think about what that means, the subtle but powerful message that sends. It's having faith that the future is brighter than the past. It's a unique approach, because so many people dwell on the past and live-in regret instead of just moving forward.

Did You Know?

- Roody is a red kangaroo. The red kangaroo is the largest species kangaroo.
- They can leap 30 feet in a single bound.
- A kangaroo's tail acts as a fifth leg so they can stand up.
- The tail also serves as a balance when they hop.
- The kangaroo is the only mammal that becomes more efficient and expends less energy the faster it moves and the more ground it covers.
- They are the most efficient animal on the planet.
- Female kangaroos are nicknamed Flyers because they're faster than males.
- Males are called Boomers because BOOM is the sound their feet make as they pound across the ground.

For additional resources visit: **CUCOroody.com**

About Chin Up Chest Out®

Roody Kangaroo Moves Forward is more than just a book to read. It is a mindset and a movement we are creating at Chin Up Chest Out® Apparel Company. Our passion is promoting mental health and that is represented in our name. Chin Up Chest Out®. It's not just a catchy slogan, it's our approach to life and our mantra. No matter what happens to you, keep your chin up, chest out and move forward.

Chin Up Chest Out® was founded in 2019 by best-selling author John Brubaker.

In 2019 Brubaker was hit with a string of injuries and that took a toll on both his physical and mental health. Spending much of the year in therapy, he began using the motto "Chin Up Chest Out®… Move Forward" to push himself and stay positive. No matter what you're going through, keep your chin up, chest out and move forward.

The phrase became more than just a reminder for him. It became a mindset in dealing with adversity and he felt it's positive impact in every area of his life. So, he wanted to share that mindset and message with the world to enable others to reap the same benefits. This was the genesis of Chin Up Chest Out® apparel company.

Our goal is to have our clothing inspire you to live life with a Chin Up Chest Out® "kangaroo mindset".

I'd like to invite you to become a member of CUCO Nation and support the brand. So, because you're reading this book if you use the promo code: **ROODY** at check out, you will receive a 20% discount on your first order plus free shipping at:

ChinUpChestOut.com

John Brubaker is a best-selling author and professional speaker. Concerned about the mental health of our youth,
John created Roody Kangaroo Moves Forward to help kids maintain a resilient, positive mindset. He is also the founder of Chin Up Chest Out Apparel Co. and CUCOradio.com
John and his wife, Bethany, live in Maine with two daughters and two Labrador retrievers. (Because Bethany wouldn't let John get kangaroos as pets.)

Piper Colston is a self-taught artist, illustrator, and aspiring story-teller. Since she was old enough to hold a pencil, Piper has been expressing herself through drawing, painting, and more recently, graphic design. She plans to study at Texas A&M University in College Station, Texas.

Made in the USA
Middletown, DE
23 July 2022